For my parents, who taught me to see and to cherish
life's miracles, and for all children who preserve
the spirit of the miraculous —J.K.

For Tessa: Merry Christmas from Mom —S.H.

Text copyright © 2022 by Jacki Kellum
Jacket art and interior illustrations copyright © 2022 by Sydney Hanson

All rights reserved. Published in the United States by Doubleday, an imprint
of Random House Children's Books, a division of Penguin Random House LLC,
New York.

Doubleday is a registered trademark and the Doubleday colophon is a trademark
of Penguin Random House LLC.

Visit us on the Web! rhcbooks.com

Educators and librarians, for a variety of teaching tools, visit us at
RHTeachersLibrarians.com

Library of Congress Cataloging-in-Publication Data
Names: Kellum, Jacki, author. | Hanson, Sydney, illustrator.
Title: The donkey's song : a Christmas nativity story / by Jacki Kellum ;
illustrated by Sydney Hanson.
Description: First edition. | New York : Doubleday Books for Young Readers,
2022. | Audience: Ages 3–6
Summary: "The story of Jesus's birth is told by the donkey that brought Mary and
Joseph to the stable in Bethlehem." —Provided by publisher.
Identifiers: LCCN 2021044133 (print) | LCCN 2021044134 (ebook) |
ISBN 978-0-593-37505-1 (hardcover) | ISBN 978-0-593-37506-8 (library binding) |
ISBN 978-0-593-37507-5 (ebook)
Subjects: LCSH: Jesus Christ—Nativity—Juvenile fiction. | Donkeys—Juvenile
fiction. | Christmas stories—Juvenile fiction. | LCGFT: Stories in rhyme.
Classification: LCC PZ8.3.K3323 Do 2022 (print) | LCC PZ8.3.K3323 (ebook) |
DDC [E]—dc23

MANUFACTURED IN CHINA
10 9 8 7 6 5 4 3 2 1
First Edition

The DONKEY'S SONG

A Christmas Nativity Story

By **Jacki Kellum**

Illustrated by **Sydney Hanson**

Doubleday Books for Young Readers

Sleepy but strong,
I clip-clopped along
to rest in a stable
with straw.

No room for a bed.
I stood near instead
and listened and
sniffed as I saw:

A bit of the forest,
a bit of its trees,
a bit of a tingle-my-toes.
That's how the evergreen
smelled to me,
a bit of fresh pine
to my nose.

A bit of a prickle,
a bit of a poke,
a flicker of warm
candlelight.

A bit of a manger,
a bit of snug hay,
a bit of a soft, silent night.

A wee-bitty Baby,
all wrapped in white cloth,
a bit of a barn gathered round.

A bit of a star,
a bit of a moon,
a bit of a sweet
angel sound.

A bit of a lamb,
all covered in fleece,
and shepherds on hills
far away.

As three wise men rode,
three presents they towed.
A bit of the night
turned to day.

All entered the stable
and circled the Babe
as sunlight beamed in
on His face.

I lifted my head
above His hay bed . . .

. . . and sang of this morning of grace.